by JOANNA COLE

pictures by JARED LEE

SCHOLASTIC INC.

New York Toronto London Auckland Sydney

ISBN 0-590-40206-4

Text copyright © 1987 by Joanna Cole
Illustrations copyright © 1987 by Jared D. Lee Studio, Inc.
All rights reserved. Published by Scholastic Inc.
Art direction by Diana Hrisinko
Book design by Emmeline Hsi

12 11 10 9 8 7 6 5 4 3 2 1   1   7 8 9/8 01 2/9

Printed in the U.S.A.   11

To Jhoneen Preece-Doswell
J.C.

To all the little monsters in the world
J.L.

Prunella was a perfect monster.
She was bad.
She growled a lot.
And she was rude
to others.

Rosie, Prunella's best friend,
was not perfect for a monster.
She was nice.
She smiled a lot.
And she was kind to everyone.

But Prunella liked her anyway.

One day, Rosie and Prunella
were sitting on the front steps,
chewing nails.

Prunella thought chewing nails
was fun.

Rosie tried to think
of something else to do.

"Let's go to
a monster movie,"
she said.

"We don't have
enough money,"
said Prunella.

"Maybe we can
earn some,"
said Rosie.

"Great idea!" said Prunella.
"We can make bug juice
and sell it."

The two friends
went to work.
Soon they had a
terrific juice stand.

Rosie smiled at everyone
who went by.

"Juice for sale!
Ten cents a cup!"
she called sweetly.

"That's no way to do it,"
said Prunella.

Prunella stood in front
of the stand.
She roared at the people.

Roaring made her thirsty.
She grabbed the pitcher
and drank it all
in one gulp.

"Uh-oh," said Prunella.
"Now we don't
   have any bug juice
   left!"

"Don't worry, Prunella,"
said Rosie.
"We don't have any customers
left, either."

"Now we can't
see the monster movie,"
said Prunella.

"Maybe we can think
of another way
to earn money,"
said Rosie.

"How about putting
on a show?"
said Prunella.

"Perfect!" said Rosie.
"Let's do
Monsterella and the Glass Sneaker."

A big audience came to see
the show.

Rosie came on stage.
She swept ashes
into the fireplace.
Everyone clapped.

Then Prunella came out.

"I'll turn this pumpkin
into a coach," Prunella said.

Prunella picked up
a big pumpkin.
She waved her
magic wand.

All of a sudden,
Prunella sniffed the pumpkin.
It smelled good enough to eat.
"Being in a play
sure makes you hungry,"
she said.

She took a big bite
of the pumpkin.

Seeds and
bits of pumpkin
went flying.

Everyone was covered
with pumpkin.

The audience got up.
They wanted
their money back.

"Just look," wailed Prunella.
"Every seat is empty."

"The money box is empty, too,"
said Rosie.

"Oh, how will we ever
get enough money to see
the movie?" Prunella said.

"Wait! I have an idea!"
Rosie said.

Rosie and Prunella
started a pet-walking service . . .

but they had to give it up.
There was too much
growling and biting
going on.

Baby-sitting didn't work out,
either.

"Maybe we can earn money
by doing chores,"
said Rosie.
"Let's ask our neighbors."

Mrs. Lampshade wanted
her windows washed.
But with Prunella around . . .

. . . the windows did not last long.

Mr. Doormat asked Rosie
and Prunella to sweep the floor.

But Prunella's broom
did not hold up.

Ms. Lawnmower needed
her fence painted.
But Prunella forgot to use
the brush.

It was almost time
for the movie.
But Rosie and Prunella
had still not
earned any money.

"What will we do?"
asked Rosie.

"Let's ask my Uncle Ned,"
said Prunella.

Uncle Ned was glad to see
Rosie and Prunella.

"I have plenty
  of work for you," he said.

Rosie carried firewood.

And Prunella chopped it.

Rosie hung laundry
on the clothesline.

Prunella dried it.

Rosie planted seeds
in the garden.

Prunella scared
the crows away.

They made a terrific team.

Soon Rosie and Prunella had enough
money to see "Invasion of the Earthworms."

They both got popcorn . . .

and they both cheered
for the earthworms.

About the Author

Joanna Cole has written more than twenty books for children. She especially likes to write about science. Some of the other books published by Scholastic are MONSTER MANNERS, BONY-LEGS, and DINOSAUR STORY. She lives in New York City with her husband, her daughter, and two dogs.

About the Artist

Jared Lee has illustrated several books for children, including MONSTER MANNERS. He has also designed posters for the U.S. Postal Service and McDonald's Restaurants. Mr. Lee lives in Lebanon, Ohio.